Echo and the Bat Pack

THE MIDNIGHT WITCHES

text by Roberto Pavanello
translated by Marco Zeni

STONE ARCH BOOKS
a capstone imprint

First published in the United States in 2012
by Stone Arch Books
A Capstone Imprint
1710 Roe Crest Drive
North Mankato, Minnesota 56003
www.capstonepub.com

Text by Roberto Pavanello
Original cover and Ilustrations by Blasco Pisapia and Pamela Brughera
Graphic Project by Laura Zuccotti and Gioia Giunchi

© 2006 Edizioni Piemme S.p.A., via Tiziano 32 – 20145 Milano- Italy
International Rights © Atlantyca S.p.A., via Leopardi, 8 — 20123 Milano, Italy — foreignrights@atlantyca.it

Original Title: STREGHE A MEZZANOTTE

Translation by: Marco Zeni

www.batpat.it

LIbrary of Congress Cataloging-in-Publication Data is available on the Library of Congress website.

ISBN: 978-1-4342-4246-4 (hardcover)
ISBN: 978-1-4342-3822-1 (library binding)

Summary: When Becca is kidnapped by an evil witch, Echo and the Bat Pack must rescue her from a terrible fate.

Designer: Emily Harris

Printed in China
0412/CA21200581
042012   006679

TABLE OF CONTENTS

CHAPTER 1: What a Swing!..8

CHAPTER 2: Writing With My Feet..17

CHAPTER 3: Becca the Movie Star..28

CHAPTER 4: The Magic Ring..35

CHAPTER 5: A Crazy Plan..43

CHAPTER 6: It's Raining Rocks!..51

CHAPTER 7: Cross-Eyed Bats..57

CHAPTER 8: Tyler's Stomach..71

CHAPTER 9: A Perfect Disguise..83

CHAPTER 10: Broom Riding..89

CHAPTER 11: How to Become a Pig..95

CHAPTER 12: The Witching Hour..104

CHAPTER 13: The Great Hundredeyes..113

CHAPTER 14: Home Sweet Home..119

HELLO THERE!

I'm your friend Echo, back again to tell you about one of the Bat Pack's adventures!

Do you know what I do for a living? I'm a writer, and scary stories are my specialty. Creepy stories about witches, ghosts, and graveyards. But I'll tell you a secret — I am a real scaredy-bat!

First of all, let me introduce you to the Bat Pack. These are my friends. . . .

Becca

Age: 10

Loves all animals (including bats, toads, and anything else gross)

An excellent actress

Michael

Age: 12

Smart, thoughtful, and good at solving problems

Doesn't take no for an answer

Tyler

Age: 11

Computer genius

Funny and adventurous, but scared of his own shadow

Dear fans of scary stories,

Who do you think is the scariest character in *Snow White*? Who's that? The queen, you say? Bingo! I agree with you. After all, the queen is the one who asked the huntsman to kill her beautiful stepdaughter, Snow White, and bring back her heart as proof that she was dead. Sounds like something out of a horror story!

What does that have to do with my story, you ask? Well, have a little patience, and I will tell you.

When she finds out that Snow White is alive, the queen transforms herself into an elderly lady and decides to pay Snow White a visit. She takes along a juicy, poisonous apple to get rid of Snow White for good!

You still can't figure out what this has to do with us? I guess I should start telling my story from the very beginning. It all started on the day I met an old lady who was selling apples. . . .

Chapter 1

What a Swing!

After my first adventure with the Silver kids, I decided to move in with the family. At first I was nervous. I was used to living alone in a crypt at the cemetery. What if I didn't like living in a house?

Just give it a shot, I thought. *I can still turn tail and go back to my tombstones.* But as it turned out, I loved it! Who would have thought that the Silvers' attic would be so comfortable for a guy used to sleeping in a moldy cemetery crypt?

Everyone in the family immediately made me feel at home. Becca put herself in charge of fashion and became my personal designer. Before I knew it, I had a pile of the coolest clothes.

I also spent a lot of time with Michael, discussing new ideas for my scary stories. He always had some good suggestions.

Tyler was usually busy playing on his computer, but he was my closest ally when it came to scary adventures. We could both be real scaredy-bats sometimes!

I was a bit nervous when the kids told their parents that I was a bat *sapiens* and that I could talk, read, and even write. Once the shock was over, though, it was all for the best. Mrs. Silver gave me an inkwell and an elegant quill. Mr. Silver was a little cautious at first, but he quickly became my friend as well. He even made a

small writing desk and a comfortable made-to-measure bed for me.

"But, Dad," Becca said, "bats sleep hanging in the air!"

"Well, then we'll fix the bed to the ceiling beam," he said.

"I'm not sure that's such a good idea," I replied. "Thank you for thinking of me, though."

Actually, I did learn to sleep lying on my back instead of hanging upside down — eventually. In the beginning, whenever I wrapped my wings tightly around my body and went to sleep, I'd fall right off the bed. But after a while, sleeping in a bed grew on me. I realized that I was also having nice dreams. I dreamed of flying. Funny, isn't it?

Don't get me wrong. I still like to sleep hanging upside down sometimes, mostly when I need to get inspiration for my stories. The blood rushing to my head always helps boost my creativity.

I was hanging upside down in the attic one afternoon, trying to get my creative juices flowing, when I was startled awake by a chilling scream. It sounded like a cat with a toothache. I listened harder, and I realized that it was a voice. Shrill and piercing, but still a voice. It was so high-pitched that I was afraid it would shatter the windows!

Who in the world is screaming like that? I wondered, trying to cover my ears. The kids were at school. Mr. Silver was at work. Only Mrs. Silver was at home, but there was no way that terrible voice belonged to her.

I let go of the beam and performed an elegant loop on my way down to the ground. Then I fluttered to the attic window to get a better look at the street below. *So much for a morning of rest!* I thought sadly. Someone should remind humans that bats like to sleep during the day.

The chilling screech shattered the quiet of Friday Street again. I looked across the street and saw a little old lady. She was wearing a tall, pointy hat and standing next to a small cart filled with fruit. I was shocked to realize that the noise had come from her.

"AAAPPLES!" the old woman screeched again. "Fresh, juicy apples, rich in vitamins and minerals! Get yours before they're gone!"

She went on like that for a full minute. It was torture! Luckily, Mrs. Silver came to the rescue. From my perch in the attic, I saw her walk out the front door of the house. With her wallet in hand, Mrs. Silver crossed the street and made her way toward the old woman.

Thank goodness, I thought. *Maybe now she'll finally stop with that awful noise.* I immediately started to fly out to thank Mrs. Silver.

Just then, the old lady turned toward the window, and I caught a glimpse of her face for the first time. Two evil eyes glinted at me from her wicked, wrinkled face. I jumped back. Scaredy-bat!

Then, just like the old hag in story of Snow

White, the woman turned to Mrs. Silver with a friendly smile, showing her the apples in her cart.

By my grandpa's sonar! Mrs. Silver was in danger — I could feel it!

Even though I was scared wingless, I knew I had to do something. Taking a deep breath, I closed my eyes and dove out the window toward the old woman. I squeaked as loud as I could to warn Mrs. Silver.

"Mrs. Silver!" I called. "You're in danger! Get away from that old witch!"

As soon as the witch noticed me, she started screeching again in her awful voice. It was useless. The more I squeaked, the louder she shrieked. My warning was completely muffled. Then the old witch took a long broom from under her cart. As soon as I was within striking distance, she swung as hard as she could. She hit me straight on and sent me flying headfirst into a lamppost.

After that, the lights went out.

Chapter 2

Writing With My Feet

When I woke up again, I was lying on the sofa in the Silvers' living room. Mrs. Silver had put an ice pack on my head and was sitting next to me with a worried look on her face.

"Are you okay, sweetheart?" she asked.

"I think so," I said. "But I feel like I was hit by a bus!"

"Well, that's what happens to you when you assault a poor, helpless old lady," she said.

"A poor, helpless old lady?" I repeated. "That woman should be playing baseball, believe me. With a swing like that she could have hit a home run!"

"Oh, that poor woman," Mrs. Silver said, shaking her head. "You scared her half to death. She just reacted."

"Did you see that old lady's face?" I asked, jumping to my feet on the couch. "She looked like a witch! Didn't you see her eyes?"

"Oh, come on, Echo!" Mrs. Silver said. (By then, she was calling me by my first name, too.) "I think you should stop writing those scary stories of yours. They've turned you into a complete scaredy-bat. You see danger everywhere! She was just a poor old woman selling fruit."

"You didn't buy anything from her, did you?" I asked.

"Of course I did!" Mrs. Silver replied. "Those apples looked delicious, and the price was too good to pass up. Would you like one?" She pointed to the basket full of delicious-looking apples sitting on the kitchen table.

"No way!" I said. "And if I were you, I wouldn't touch them either."

"Why on earth not?" she asked.

I hesitated. I didn't have any actual proof, just a feeling. But my feelings were rarely wrong. "Because something is wrong," I said. "I can't explain it. I just *feel* it."

Mrs. Silver looked at me skeptically. My argument hadn't exactly convinced her. "Echo, you're imagining things," she told me. "Look, I'll prove there's nothing wrong with these apples."

Mrs. Silver stood up and went into the kitchen. She picked up an apple off the table and

took a huge bite. Nothing happened.

"Are you convinced now?" she asked. I wasn't, but I had to face the facts. I didn't have any proof.

At five o'clock, Michael, Becca, and Tyler came home from school, and the house was once again full of activity. Finally! I had begun to miss it. I quickly flew over to the front door.

"Hey, Echo! How's it going?" Tyler said, high-fiving me so hard that he sent me spinning. While I was still reeling from his greeting, Tyler hurried into the kitchen to fix himself an after-school snack.

Michael waved a brand-new book under my nose as he walked by. The cover showed an enormous white rabbit with glowing eyes. "Check this out, Echo!" he said. "I've been waiting for this for months!"

"What is it?" I asked.

"It's the new book by Edgar Allan Poultry," Michael explained. "It's called *The Revenge of the Giant Rabbit*. I'll let you borrow it as soon as I'm finished reading it!" With that, Michael ran upstairs and disappeared into his bedroom. I knew I wouldn't be seeing him again for a while.

Becca was the only one who seemed to sense that something wasn't quite right. She stopped and stared at me.

"Is everything okay?" she asked.

I hesitated for a moment. "Yeah, fine," I said. "What about you? How was school today?"

"It was okay. Come on, Echo, I can tell something's bugging you," Becca said.

I wasn't sure that telling her about my suspicions was such a good idea, but keeping something from Becca is like trying to hide an elephant behind a mouse. I gave in and told her what had happened that morning — every single detail.

Becca listened to my story without interruption. But when I told her my theory about the old woman and the apples, she burst out laughing.

"What's so funny?" I asked, somewhat hurt.

"Nothing, nothing," she replied. "It's just a funny coincidence."

"What's the coincidence?" I asked.

"The principal announced a competition today at school," she explained. "We have to write our own ending to *Snow White and the Seven Dwarfs*. With your imagination, you should enter the contest."

Becca giggled again. "I can see it already," she continued. "'The evil witch approached, offering an apple to the princess as a reward for her kindness, when a brave bat interfered and saved the day. The witch, brandishing a broom, chased the bat down and sent him soaring into a lamppost.' How's that?"

"Very funny!" I said. I was about to tell Becca to just forget it. Clearly, she wasn't taking me seriously. But just then, Tyler appeared at the top of the stairs.

"Echo, come upstairs!" he called. "I got it!"

"Got what?" I asked, but Tyler had already disappeared.

We followed him to his bedroom. Michael was lying on his bed, so deep into his new book that he didn't even realize we were there.

"I finally figured out how you can use the computer!" Tyler explained.

"Tyler, I already told you . . ." I began.

"I know, I know," he said. "You have wings attached to your hands."

"Exactly," I agreed.

"But not to your feet, right?" Tyler asked. He leaned back in his desk chair and put his bare feet on the keyboard. To my surprise, he used his toes to type several error-free sentences. Even Michael stopped reading to watch.

"See?" Tyler said. "All it took was a couple of

days of training. And with my hands free, I can keep eating my chips!" He stuck his hand back in the bag. "What do you think?"

"Well, someday, someone could say that my stories are so bad that it looks like I used my feet to write them," I replied. "And they'd be right." And with that, I went back up to the attic.

Chapter 3

Becca the Movie Star

When Mrs. Silver called us down to dinner, I was the last one to go.

I wasn't very hungry, and I was a little worried that Mrs. Silver would tell everyone about what had happened that afternoon with the old lady. I was starting to feel a little silly, to tell you the truth. Maybe I had overreacted.

Luckily, though, Mrs. Silver kept the afternoon's events a secret. Becca didn't say a word about it either. Instead, she chattered on about the Snow White competition. Soon, the whole family was trying to come up with a story.

"How about the prince is a computer expert, and with help from Snow White and the dwarfs, he creates a game where you have to hunt the witch," Tyler suggested. "Then the game is nominated for an international contest and wins first prize. They all get rich, and the prince turns the castle into an amusement park for kids. Pretty good, right?"

"Get real, Tyler," Michael said. "You can't turn a fairy tale into a science-fiction story. Am I right, Echo? How would *you* change the ending? Tell us."

I wasn't surprised Michael asked my opinion. Thanks to the old librarian who'd taught me how to read and write, I knew a lot of stories. But I had never heard of Snow White or her seven dwarfs. I was just about to confess that I was clueless when Mrs. Silver put a basket full of apples on the table. The same apples she had bought that morning.

My ears started buzzing. Something terrible was going to happen if they ate those apples — I could feel it! But then again, nothing had happened to Mrs. Silver when she'd eaten one earlier. I tried to remain calm. Maybe my confession about Snow White would distract everyone from the apples. I decided to give it a shot.

"I . . . um . . . actually, I've never heard of *Snow White and the Seven Dwarfs*," I said.

There was a moment of silence.

"Are you serious?" Becca asked. "How is that even possible?"

"I don't know. Maybe my librarian hated

apples," I said, eying the basket nervously. So far, no one had touched it.

"Well, I guess we'll have to tell you the story, then," Becca said. "Once upon a time, there was a beautiful queen. . . ."

Everyone listened as Becca began to tell the story of Snow White. I listened too, but I never took my eyes off the basket of apples on the table.

By the time Becca got to the part where the witch offers Snow White the poisoned apple, we were all captivated by the tale. Becca picked up a juicy red apple from the basket to use as a prop.

"Then the girl put the poisoned apple to her mouth," Becca said, "and bit into it." Becca put the apple to her lips and took a huge bite. She let out a muffled scream and collapsed on the floor.

The Silver family clapped loudly. Even I cheered. Her performance had been flawless.

Tyler stood up and whistled. "Bravo! Encore!" he yelled.

"She should be an actress," Mr. Silver said. "I've always thought that."

"Go on, dear," Mrs. Silver said to Becca. "Finish the story. It doesn't end that tragically."

But Becca didn't respond. She continued to lay motionless on the floor. It took everyone a minute to realize she wasn't joking. Something was very wrong.

I gasped. I couldn't believe I'd been so distracted by Becca's acting that I'd forgotten about the apples.

"It was the apple!" I yelled.

Mrs. Silver looked at me, horrified. "We

have to take her to the hospital immediately!"
she cried.

Two minutes later, the whole Silver family
was on its way to Fogville's ER. Becca was lying
on the backseat. As we raced to the hospital, I
held Becca's hand. It was as cold as ice.

Chapter 4

The Magic Ring

When we arrived at Fogville Hospital, Becca was immediately rushed into an exam room. I stayed hidden in Tyler's jacket pocket while Mr. and Mrs. Silver told the ER doctor what had happened.

When they were finished, the doctor stared at them in shock. "Is this some kind of joke?" he asked. "Are you in on it with the other family?"

"What do you mean?" Michael asked.

"What I mean is that your sister is the second girl to come in tonight with these symptoms," he explained. "It seems that someone in Fogville has been selling rotten fruit to people."

The doctor turned back to Mr. and Mrs. Silver. "We'll have to pump Becca's stomach and hope it helps," he said.

"What do you mean, 'hope it helps'?" Mrs. Silver said. "What happened to your other patient? The girl who came in earlier tonight?"

"I didn't mean to scare you," the doctor said. "The other patient seems to be okay. But the thing is . . ."

"The thing is *what?*" Mrs. Silver asked, sounding alarmed.

"Well, it seems that she's unable to recognize her family," the doctor said. "She looks at them and smiles, but it's like she doesn't really see them."

I listened to everything from my hiding place inside Tyler's jacket. "I knew it!" I muttered. "I knew something was wrong. 'Poor old lady' my foot!"

"I'm sure your daughter will be okay," the doctor assured the Silvers as a nurse whisked Becca away. "Don't worry."

They made us wait outside the emergency room for an hour. When they brought Becca back out of the room, Mr. and Mrs. Silver dashed toward the doctor, desperate for information. Michael and Tyler and I followed the nurse, who was pushing Becca, in a wheelchair, into another room.

As we entered the room, I stuck my head out of Tyler's pocket to take a peek around. They'd put Becca in the same room as another patient. A very skinny little girl with short hair sat on the other bed. Her legs were stiff and she was staring blankly into the distance. I figured she must be the other girl the doctor had mentioned earlier.

"Psst!" Tyler whispered to Michael.

"What?" his brother replied.

"That girl is giving me the creeps," Tyler whispered, nodding toward the other bed. "Look at her eyes!"

"Hi!" Michael said, trying to get the girl's attention. "I'm Michael. What's your name?"

The girl slowly turned her head and barely smiled at him. Then she went back to staring off into the distance silently.

"Nice. A girl of few words," Tyler commented, turning back to his brother.

Just then, my foot snagged on something in Tyler's pocket. "What on earth?" I said, trying to yank free. Tyler quickly fished me out of his pocket. I was holding a small ring with a red stone.

"Echo, you're a genius!" he yelled, giving me a quick hug. "I couldn't find that anywhere!"

"What's that supposed to be?" Michael asked.

"It's a *magic* ring, my present for Becca," Tyler explained. "I meant to give it to her for her birthday."

"But her birthday was three months ago," Michael said.

"Okay, so I'm a little late," Tyler said. "It's the thought that counts, right?" As I watched, he walked over to Becca's hospital bed, where she lay with her eyes closed, and slipped the ring on her finger.

Suddenly, Mr. and Mrs. Silver came back with the doctor. Tyler couldn't put me away in time.

"What's that . . . that . . . thing?" the doctor stuttered, pointing at me.

"He's not a thing," Michael said defensively. "He's a bat!"

"Well, I can see that," the doctor said, "but it shouldn't be in a hospital!"

Luckily, Mrs. Silver stepped in. "Echo is part of the family and one of Becca's best friends," she told the doctor.

"He and Becca are always together," Mr. Silver agreed. "They're practically inseparable."

"Well, they won't be able to stay together tonight," the doctor replied. "Only one parent can stay with her. Tomorrow —"

Just then, a very alarmed looking nurse poked her head into the room and interrupted us. "Doctor, you'd better come quickly!" she said.

"It looks like another girl ate one of those rotten apples."

"Unbelievable!" the doctor said. "Is this some kind of epidemic?" With that, he dashed down the hall, his coat flapping at his sides.

The family decided that Mrs. Silver would stay overnight at the hospital with Becca, and Mr. Silver would take Michael, Tyler, and me home. Before leaving, we all leaned down and kissed Becca goodbye. She didn't even stir.

When it was his turn, Tyler whispered something in Becca's ear, as if she could hear him. But before I could ask what he'd told her, we were quickly ushered from the room.

Chapter 5

A Crazy Plan

No one slept well in the Silver house that night. I tossed and turned in my new bed. I couldn't stop worrying about Becca. I finally fell asleep near dawn, but even then I had awful nightmares. I dreamed that Snow White was chasing me around the dwarfs' house, yelling, "A rat! A rat!" and trying to hit me with a broom.

In my dream the telephone rang, and Snow White answered it. She had the voice of a man and was talking so loud that she woke me up. "Gone?!" she cried.

I awoke with a start. That wasn't Snow White on the telephone. It was Mr. Silver, and he was talking to his wife.

Michael, Tyler, and I all stumbled out of our rooms and downstairs. My eyes were bleary, Michael didn't have his glasses on, and Tyler was in his underwear.

"What do you mean, she's gone?" Mr. Silver cried. "Are you sure? Yes, I'm on my way right now!" He hung up  the phone and stared at us, dumbfounded. "Becca disappeared! And so did both of the other girls that were at the hospital with her."

"Did someone call the police?" Michael asked. As usual, he was the one who stayed calm.

"Yes, of course," his father said. "I'm going to the hospital. You three stay here. The police might call if they know something. If you hear anything, let me know immediately! I'm counting on you three!"

"Okay, Mr. Silver," I answered. "We'll do everything we can."

Mr. Silver got dressed in a hurry and rushed out of the house wearing a pair of mismatched shoes.

After Mr. Silver had gone, I sat down at the breakfast table with the two boys, but nobody was hungry. We turned on the television and saw that the morning news was already reporting the story.

Just then I noticed that Michael's glasses had

fogged up. Bad sign. That always meant that trouble was on its way.

The phone suddenly rang. Michael picked it up quickly. Then he handed me the receiver. "It's for you."

"H-hello?" I said into the receiver. It was the very first time that I used that gizmo! "Who is this?"

"Echo, it's me, Mrs. Silver," she said. Through the phone I could hear her crying. "Oh, you were right. Something was terribly wrong with those apples. I'm sorry! If only I had listened to you."

"It doesn't matter now," I said quickly. "We have to concentrate on finding Becca. You can count on me. I'll hunt down that evil old witch!"

When I hung up the phone, I realized that Tyler and Michael were staring at me in shock.

"Since when do you hunt down evil old witches?" Tyler asked.

"There's something you haven't told us," Michael said. "Come on, spill your guts."

I realized that the boys still didn't know the full story. I figured I should start at the beginning. I told them about the previous day, from when I'd first seen the old woman selling her apples, to getting hit with a broom, to the moment Becca had taken a bite of the apple. When I had finished, they were even more confused.

"This is crazy!" Tyler said. "So you're saying that old lady cast a spell on those girls with the apples and then kidnapped them?"

"I'd bet my right wing on it!" I said.

"If that's really the case, then all we have to do is find her!" Tyler exclaimed. "Case closed!"

"Yeah, right," Michael said sarcastically. "All

we have to do is comb the entire city of Fogville, hope the woman hasn't left town yet, and that's it. Piece of cake."

"Or . . . we could use the *magic ring*!" Tyler said with a sneaky smile.

"How can you joke about this?" Michael asked. "Our sister is missing!"

"I'm not joking," Tyler told him. "Do you remember the little ring that I gave Becca at the hospital? It's no ordinary ring. It's my latest invention, *the pager-ring*!"

"What is that supposed to mean?" Michael asked.

"It means that when someone gets lost, all he has to do is turn the ring around his finger, and the ring will send a signal to the receiver," Tyler explained. "It makes finding a missing person a piece of cake!"

"So where exactly is this receiver?" Michael asked. He was starting to sound a bit more interested in his brother's plan.

"Right here!" Tyler said, placing a small metal box with a thin antenna on the table.

Michael sighed. "How is Becca supposed to even know how the ring works?" he asked.

"I whispered that to her yesterday, a few seconds before we left her room," Tyler told us proudly.

"Let me get this straight," Michael said. "You told Becca how this magic ring invention of yours works when she couldn't hear you?"

"Exactly!" Tyler replied, smiling.

Michael and I exchanged a puzzled look. He shrugged. It might not have been a great plan, but for the moment, it was the only one we had.

Chapter 6

It's Raining Rocks!

The whole day went by, and there was still no news about Becca or the other two girls. The apple lady had vanished into thin air.

"I'll bet my left wing that she isn't even in town anymore!" I said.

"You'd better be careful, Echo," Tyler said. "If you keep betting wings, you won't be able to fly!"

When Mr. and Mrs. Silver came home that night, we still hadn't heard anything. The police had no clues. And Tyler's plan had gotten us nowhere. The receiver for the magic ring had been silent all afternoon.

When the rest of the family went to bed, I decided to take a quick night flight to clear my head. Maybe I'd be able to uncover some new information. The night was clear and beautiful. I was so happy to have my wings that I swore I would never bet them again!

I flew to the outskirts of Fogville and perched on a branch. I was so worried about Becca. *Where are you, Becca?* I wondered. *Send us a signal, and we'll come and get you.*

Unfortunately, my exploration didn't unearth any new information. We were still no closer to finding Becca or the other missing girls. With a sigh, I turned to fly home, empty-winged. I was about to fly back in the attic window when I saw two shadows standing by the front door. Burglars!

I knew I had to do something, but I was so scared that my wings were shaking. Suddenly I remembered one of the tricks my cousin Limp Wing, a member of the aerobatic display team, had taught me — rock bombs!

I knew I had to give it a try. I grabbed a rock the size of an egg from the garden and used my little wings to raise it high into the air. I took aim at the bigger burglar and let go. The rock hit the burglar right on the head. Bullseye!

"Ouch!" he yelled, covering his head. "It's raining rocks!"

I picked up another rock and took aim for my second shot. This time I hit the other burglar on the shoulder. Direct hit!

I flew down to pick up another rock, but when I looked around the burglars had disappeared. That was close! I thought. I flew back into the open attic window and headed for my little bed. Suddenly, two powerful arms grabbed me and covered my mouth. Someone turned on the light, blinding me.

"Since when is it okay to throw rocks at your friends?" a familiar voice asked.

"Michael! Tyler!" I said. "That was you? I thought you were two burglars!"

"I should have remembered that bats have terrible sight," Tyler said, rubbing his head.

"Why were you outside in the middle of the night?" I asked.

"Because we finally saw this," Michael said. He held out a small metal box. I stared at it for a second before realizing what it was.

The receiver.

Tyler's invention was coming in handy after all. On top of the box, a red light now blinked steadily.

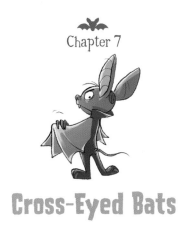

Chapter 7

Cross-Eyed Bats

Michael, Tyler, and I tiptoed out of the house silently. We were already at the end of Friday Street when Michael stopped dead in his tracks.

"I forgot something!" he said. Before we could stop him, Michael turned around and darted back toward the Silvers' house. He was back a minute later, carrying a small backpack.

"Okay, we can go now," he said.

Neither Tyler nor I asked him what was in the backpack. Knowing Michael, I figured it had to be something important. -

"Why do all of our adventures have to take place at night?" Tyler complained. "Can't we ever solve a mystery during the day?"

"Stop complaining and tell us where we're going," Michael told him. "How does that receiver work?"

"It depends on the strength of the signal coming from the ring," Tyler said, studying the

receiver. "The closer she is, the brighter the light gets."

"Okay, you lead the way," Michael said. "This is your invention, after all."

Following the signal on the receiver, we headed for the outskirts of Fogville. At the end of the road, we found ourselves facing the entrance to a dark forest. Glancing up, I recognized the tree branch I'd been perched on earlier that night. Maybe I'd actually picked up a distress signal from Becca on my night exploration.

"Where does this street go?" Tyler asked uncertainly.

"Toward the Red Oak Woods, I think," I replied. "Not a very nice place."

"Why do you say that?" Tyler asked.

"Well, rumor has it that many have gone into the woods," I explained. "But very few come back out."

"Did you hear that, Michael?" Tyler said. "Let's go back."

"We can't go back," Michael said. "Our sister is in there. Do you want to save Becca or not?"

"Of course I do," Tyler answered. "But . . ."

"But what?" Michael said impatiently.

"But do Echo and I have permission to be scared?" Tyler asked.

"Fine," Michael said. "Can we go in now?"

All three of us stepped into the woods. After just a few steps, we were completely swallowed by darkness. We bats love the dark, but this was something else. The crooked branches of the old oak trees looked like skeleton arms ready to reach out and grab us.

Michael turned on a flashlight to guide the way. I had my sonar, which let me see what was around us, even in the pitch-black night. At least I thought I could see. I was fluttering warily through the air when I was suddenly hit by a group of fellow bats that were speeding in the opposite direction. I was quickly swept up in the swarm.

"Beat it!" one of them exclaimed.

"Why are you flying so fast?" I asked. "Where are you going?"

"Hundredeyes is coming!" one of the bats answered, panting for breath. "If he catches you, you're done for!"

"Hundredeyes?" I repeated. "Who's that?" Nobody answered. Instead, the colony of bats split up, each one flying in a different direction.

One little fellow lagged behind. He must have been exhausted and scared, because he started to cry, flapping his trembling little wings.

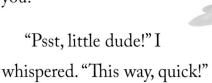

"Mommy!" he cried. "Mommy, where are you?"

"Psst, little dude!" I whispered. "This way, quick!"

The little bat followed me into the hollowed-out trunk of a dead tree without hesitation. Peeking my head out of the hideout, I saw a huge bat coming our way. He stopped in midair and scanned the area around us, glaring menacingly in every direction.

Even though I was feeling pretty scared, I almost burst out laughing when I realized that he was completely cross-eyed and wore a long orange pom-pom hat. He looked left and right for the last time and then flew back the same way he'd come.

"Was that Hundredeyes?" I asked the little bat.

"Yes," he whispered in a feeble voice.

"Why is he so dangerous?" I asked.

"He's Circe's helper," he answered.

"Circe?" I asked. "Who's that?"

"She's an evil witch!" the little bat exclaimed. "She has a hideout here in the forest. Hundredeyes helps guard it."

"A witch?" I repeated. *It must be the same woman I saw selling apples in Fogville*, I thought. *The one who has Becca!*

"Do you know where that hideout is?" I asked.

"Oh, that's easy," the bat replied. "Keep going straight, and you'll see an enormous rock. It's right next to the entrance of a cave. You can't go in, though. My granddad says that the real entrance is hidden."

"Did he tell you where it is?" I asked.

"No sir, he says it's too dangerous," the bat said, shaking his head. "You don't want to go there, do you?"

"I don't want to, but I have to," I told him. "That witch has kidnapped one of my friends. I have to help her." I peered around to make sure Hundredeyes was gone. "It looks like the coast is clear. I think you'd better go back to your mother now."

"Goodbye!" the little bat said. He shot out of the trunk and fluttered away. "Thank you for your help, sir!"

I quickly flew out of the trunk and made my way back to Michael and Tyler. By the time I reached them, the receiver was beeping steadily and flashing brightly.

"There you are, Echo! I thought we'd lost you! We're getting closer. Did you find anything?" Michael asked.

"I ran into a very helpful little bat," I said. "He said that if we go this way, we'll find the entrance to a cave. Becca is there . . . with the witch."

"W-witch?" Tyler stuttered.

"Circe," I told him. "That's her name."

"Let's just stay on this path," Michael suggested. "It has to lead somewhere."

Michael was right. After just a few minutes of walking, we found the enormous rock the little bat had described. The three of us stopped in front of the stone wall that hid the entrance to the cave. We found an opening.

"What now?" Tyler asked.

"Well, Echo could fly in quickly and investigate," Michael suggested.

"Great idea!" Tyler said. "Echo, you go on in, and we'll wait for you out here. Take your time."

I was about to protest. Why did I have to be the one to go in and investigate? But then I remembered that Becca was in there. She was my friend. I had to be brave if I was going to save her from the witch!

"Okay," I said. "I'll fly in and take a look around."

"Be careful," Michael said. "And quiet."

With that, I flew into the cave. Unfortunately,

I didn't get very far. The darkness had been hiding a solid stone wall that blocked the way. I flew straight into it. And then it was lights out for me.

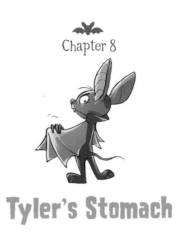

Chapter 8

Tyler's Stomach

When I came to, Michael and Tyler were staring at me with worried expressions.

"What happened?" I asked, massaging my head. "Am I dead?"

"You're alive. You just didn't see this," Michael replied, tapping on a granite wall.

How come my sonar didn't detect it? Could the witch have something to do with it?

"We obviously can't go in this way," Michael observed. "Any ideas?"

"Oh, shoot! I guess I'm all out of dynamite!" Tyler said, showing his empty pockets.

"Very funny!" Michael said. Then he turned back to me. "Echo, would you mind taking another look?"

"Again? That's not fair!" I said. "Why can't one of you go?"

"Tyler and I can't fly," Michael said. "We don't have any way to get in there. Think of Becca! Do it for her!"

I thought of Becca . . . and of Hundredeyes, too. I really didn't want to run into him. But I knew Becca was counting on me.

Taking a deep breath, I flew up and over the top of the cave. Suddenly, the baby bat's words came back to me: "My granddad says that the real way in is hidden." I used my sonar and was happy to see that it was still working perfectly. In just a few minutes I found what I was looking for. I flew back down to Michael and Tyler to tell them the good news.

"The entrance is on the top of the mountain," I told them. "We have to go up there."

"Climb all the way up there?" Tyler cried. "But I'm exhausted!"

"Okay, then you can stay here," Michael said.

"You keep watch in front of the main entrance. Let us know if the witch comes out."

"I don't want to stay here alone!" Tyler said quickly. "On second thought, I love mountain climbing!"

It took a lot longer to get to the top of the mountain this time, since Michael and Tyler couldn't fly. When they finally made it to the top, we found a very narrow opening.

"My foot won't even fit in there!" Tyler said.

"Maybe I can squeeze my leg through that hole," Michael said, looking at me from behind his glasses. "Echo, could you —"

Here we go again! I thought. This was the third time those two had asked me to risk my life! I wanted to say no, but I couldn't fail Becca.

Holding my breath, I squeezed into the dark, narrow tunnel. It was a very tight fit. There was no way Michael or Tyler would have made it through.

Suddenly, the tunnel opened up into a huge candlelit cavern. A muddy pond full of croaking toads covered the bottom of the cave. On a raised island in the center of the pond, I finally saw Becca. She was sitting as still as a statue. The only movement she made was to twist Tyler's ring.

That must be how she activated the signal! I thought.

The skinny girl we'd seen at the hospital sat next to Becca, along with another girl. They both seemed frozen in place.

In front of the three girls stood a woman dressed in long, ratty robes. A tall pointed hat covered her snarled hair. It was the apple lady — or should I say Circe, the witch!

Circe raised her arm in a threatening gesture, and the toads fell silent.

"Dear friends," she screeched. "We are gathered here today to choose my new assistant. I need a new one. I had to retire old Ludmilla because of her inadequacies!"

She shot a bolt of lightning from her wand at a sad-looking toad. *That must be Ludmilla*, I thought.

"I sincerely hope that one of you three will be the one I am looking for," Circe continued. "As for the other two, you will increase the number of my beloved subjects by being transformed into two strapping young toads! Ha ha ha!"

The toads started croaking so loudly that I had to cover my ears.

"Silence!" the witch said. "At midnight sharp, the forces of magic will show me the chosen one. Let the ceremony begin!"

I glanced at the glowing face of my digital watch (a gift from Tyler). It was already 11:45 — only fifteen minutes to midnight! There wasn't enough time for me to go back and tell Michael and Tyler what was happening. Even if I was shaking like a pile of jelly, I had to do something. But what?

Then I remembered something my cousin Limp Wing always used to say. "Desperate times call for desperate aerobatic measures!" I decided to attempt the most difficult maneuver he had taught me — the nosedive!

Taking a deep breath, I plunged at full speed toward Becca. I hit her in her right shoulder, knocking her off balance. We both tumbled to the ground. I hoped the fall would be enough to make Becca wake up and recognize me.

But the opposite happened. Becca didn't seem to recognize me at all. In fact, she started screaming and swatting me away! The noise caught the witch's attention.

"Hundredeyes!" she bellowed. "Tear him apart!"

The cross-eyed bat materialized out of thin air and bolted toward me. Scaredy-bat! I dashed toward the opposite end of the cave and found myself in a pitch-black tunnel. Not giving it a second thought, I flew in. Hundredeyes was hot on my heels.

"I'll have your ears as appetizers, buddy!" I heard him holler from behind me.

I tried to ignore him. I was busy trying to figure out where that tunnel would end. When I finally did, it was too late. The same granite wall I had rammed into earlier was right in front of me!

I was so desperate that I managed to perform an incredible loop in that tiny little space! Hundredeyes said just two words: "*Secretum passageum!*"

The wall opened, and Hundredeyes flew through it safe and sound. Or almost safe and sound. He hadn't been expecting to hit Tyler on the other side.

Chapter 9

A Perfect Disguise

"What are you two doing here?" I asked Michael and Tyler. Both boys were staring at Hundredeyes, who was unconscious on the ground.

"Michael wanted me to stay up on top of the cave, where you flew in, while he checked out the other entrance," Tyler explained.

"But the poor baby was getting dizzy up there on his own," Michael added, shaking his head. "So here we are."

"Well, at least the three of us are together again! Tyler said. "Actually, the four of us. Who's the guy who crashed into me?"

"That's Hundredeyes," I explained. "He's the witch's helper. We'd better tie him up. He's pretty dangerous."

"Dangerous?" Michael repeated. He stared at the cross-eyed bat. Hundredeyes was still wearing his orange pom-pom hat. I had to admit, he didn't exactly look dangerous at the moment.

I quickly told them what I had seen in the cave. When they heard that Becca and the other two girls were being held inside, Michael and Tyler both looked relieved. We'd found them! But we weren't out of danger yet. We still had to get the girls out of there . . . and away from the witch.

"I think I have an idea," Michael said. "Hundredeyes opened the entrance to the cave, right?"

"Right," I said. "And I saw how he did it. Watch this."

Turning to face the wall, I repeated the words I'd heard Hundredeyes say. "*Secretum passageum!*"

As we watched in amazement, the granite wall in front of us magically opened.

"Echo, you're a wizard!" Tyler exclaimed, looking impressed.

"Well," I said bashfully, "let's just say that I have good ears!"

"Okay, Echo," Michael said. "You go back in there and pretend to be Hundredeyes. The witch will assume you took care of the trouble and that her assistant is still alive. Then Tyler and I will sneak in behind you and set Becca free. Got it?"

"There's just one problem," I said. "How am I supposed to pretend to be cross-eyed?"

"Leave that to us," Michael said. While Tyler tied up Hundredeyes, Michael went to work on me. He spattered dirt all over me and put Hundredeyes' hat on my head. Since I couldn't cross my eyes, no matter how hard I tried, Michael gave me a pair of sunglasses.

"If the witch asks, just say you took them from the other bat," he told me. "You'll be okay."

"I hope so!" I said. To tell you the truth, I was scared wingless! But to save Becca, I would have slept downside up!

As Michael, Tyler, and I walked through the tunnel, I asked the question that had been bothering me for a while. "How are we going to free Becca?"

Michael took off his backpack. "I brought some supplies," he said, opening the bag.

"Hey! That's my stuff!" Tyler exclaimed, as soon as he saw what was in the backpack. "Where did you get it?"

"Your closet," Michael said. "Now let's see if it works."

"My inventions always work," Tyler said. "You should know that by now."

Chapter 10

Broom Riding

When Michael finished explaining his plan, I felt a little better. Maybe there was a way out of this mess after all.

"Come on, Echo!" Michael said. "We're counting on you!"

My heart was pounding so loudly when I flew into the cave that I was sure the witch would hear it. But she didn't even look at me.

"Did you get him?" she asked.

"Made mincemeat of him!" I replied. I flew over to the side of the cave and landed in a dark nook where I could hide.

"Well done, Hundredeyes!" Circe screeched. "Double portion of toad soup for you tonight!"

Yuck! That made me sick!

The witch turned to her young prisoners. "And now, my dear girls, let us begin with the first of the two trials you shall undergo," she said. "It is a classic test all witches must pass — the broom ride! Pay attention!"

Circe climbed aboard her broom and flew to the top of the cave. Then she performed a nosedive and an aerobatic loop before skimming across the water. Even Limp Wing himself would have applauded. The toads croaked enthusiastically.

"Thank you! Thank you!" the old woman said smugly. She walked back toward the girls. "Now, who wishes to go first?"

Staring blankly into the distance, Becca stepped forward.

"Excellent!" the witch said, handing her the broom. "I have to warn you, my dear, the trial I've created for you is going to be slightly more difficult." Pointing toward the center of the pond, Circe yelled, "*Focus!*" Immediately, a big ring caught on fire.

"All you have to do is fly through the ring of fire. Only once," Circe said. "It's quite simple, really. Ride this broom, and prove to me that you're a real witch!"

I was terrified. With one eye, I watched Becca balance on the broom. With the other, I watched the tunnel where Michael and Tyler were supposed to pop up. A couple more minutes and my eyes would cross for real!

Becca started flying up and down the cave, grazing the walls dangerously. It looked like she had been doing that forever! Was she a real witch after all?

"Good! Excellent!" the witch screeched. "The ring of fire, now!"

Just then, Michael and Tyler came out of the tunnel and saw their sister taking a nosedive toward the flames. "BECCA, NOOOOOO!" Tyler shouted.

Furious, the witch turned to face the boys. She fired a blue lightning bolt right at Tyler. Direct hit! Michael tried to run, but Circe quickly immobilized him with another lightning bolt from her wand.

"Hundredeyes!" she shouted. "Who are they?"

"I . . . I have no idea . . ." I mumbled, crawling out of my hideout. Circe was tying up my friends! I felt terrible, but for the time being, there was nothing I could do to save Michael and Tyler.

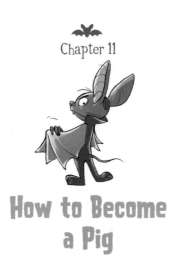

Chapter 11

How to Become
a Pig

Despite all the commotion, Becca had landed safe and sound on her broom. She stared at me blankly.

"Where in the world did you get those ridiculous sunglasses?" the witch asked me.

"I took them from the bat I liquefied," I told her. "It was clear that he was working with those boys."

"And how is it possible that they managed to

get in?" the witch bellowed. "Huh? You didn't let anyone hear the magic word, did you?"

The witch didn't wait for me to answer before unleashing hundreds of lightning bolts at me. I managed to duck the first few and flew into the tunnel to hide. But just when I thought I was safe — *ZAP!* I instantly fell to the ground.

"I'll deal with you later!" I heard Circe yell. That was the last thing I heard before I passed out.

Luckily, the witch didn't worry about Hundredeyes — that is, me — for a while. When I came to I was dizzy, but I managed to crawl to the end of the tunnel. The three girls were back on the island in the center of the cave. Michael and Tyler were still lying on the ground where the witch had left them.

"Excellent! We now have a couple of guinea pigs on which to practice my spells!" the witch said. "That is lucky, isn't it, my dears?"

The little girls kept staring ahead, icy and expressionless.

"Let us forget the brooms and take advantage of these two young lads for the following trial!" Circe continued, bolts shooting from her eyes. "I learned the following spell from my grandmother — it was one of her specialties. Watch closely, girls!"

Circe pointed her long wand at two toads and began chanting:

"Darkness, lightning bolts, and fright,

Fill the air with hazy light.

Study the animals one by one,

And turn each into a pig, just for fun!"

When Circe finished, there was a puff of white smoke. When it cleared, two pink pigs stood where the toads had been.

"Ha ha ha! It's always as fun as the first time!" the old hag said with a grin. "And now, my dears, it is your turn to try . . . on them!" She pointed to Michael and Tyler, who were starting to wake up.

The short-haired girl picked up the wand and pointed it at Michael and Tyler. With glazed eyes, she started reciting the spell Circe had just used.

Tyler tried to distract her. "Hey, hi there!" he said. "Do you know how a hog gets fat? He eats like a . . . pig! You're not laughing? It was a good one, though — hey, wait!"

She didn't wait. A puff of white smoke clouded the air again.

"Hey! Look what you've done to me!" Tyler complained, pointing at the corkscrew tail sticking out of his pants.

"Hush!" the witch bellowed. "Or I'll turn you into a ham! Your turn," she said to the other girl. "Hurry up! It's almost midnight!"

The other girl recited the spell again. But when the white smoke cleared, only Tyler was turned into a pig!

"It's not enough! It's not enough!" the witch said angrily. "Both boys at the same time!"

Circe muttered something, and Tyler became human again. "Come on, little girl," Circe said, turning to Becca. "It's your turn now. If you pass this test, you will have the privilege of becoming my assistant! Don't disappoint me!"

Becca picked up the wand, and stared at her brothers blankly.

"Becca, fight it," Michael pleaded. "Please!"

"Becca, come on, we're your brothers! Can't you see that?" Tyler yelled.

"Well, well, well," the witch said, getting closer. "What have we here? My future assistant's brothers! What an honor! In that case, I won't make sausage and bacon out of you two after all. Consider your lives spared!"

"Are you serious?" Tyler asked, full of hope. "You're not going to kill us?"

"Why should I?" Circe said with an evil grin.

"You two will make beautiful toads to add to my collection! Ha ha ha! Let us proceed!"

Becca stepped closer. In a few moments, I would lose my friends forever!

Then I noticed something. Michael wasn't carrying his backpack!

He must have lost it in the tunnel when he was trying to run away, I realized.

That meant that it might still be near me. Maybe we still had hope after all!

I crawled backward down the tunnel for a few steps until I spotted the backpack. Inside was Tyler's latest invention, smoke strings. It was a gadget 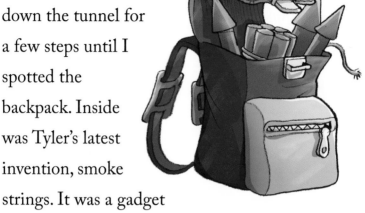 he'd created for Halloween. It shot silly string made of colored smoke. Useful, huh?

"These things make such a mess," Michael had said when explaining his plan. "Mom and Dad hated when we used them in the house. But they'll work perfectly here. By the time the witch realizes that we got in, we'll already be gone!"

I hoped he was right. I quickly set Tyler's contraptions on the floor and pointed them toward the cave. From inside, I could hear the witch encouraging Becca to recite the spell. I knew I had to move quickly. I was running out of time!

I fumbled through the bag, looking for the last thing I needed, the most important one. A match. There were none.

We were done for.

Chapter 12

The Witching Hour

Then, from behind me, I heard a threatening voice.

"Give me back my hat!" Hundredeyes said.

"Hundredeyes!" I said. "How did you break free?"

"Piece of cake for a witch's assistant," he told me. "I've been Circe's assistant for a while now, and I've learned a thing or two!"

"I guess you're going to take me to your

master now, huh?" I asked. It seemed I had reached the end of the road.

Hundredeyes came closer, a serious look on his face. Well, as serious as a cross-eyed bat can look, anyway. Then he snatched his orange pom-pom hat from my head.

"Dear friend, I must thank you," he said.

"*Thank me?*" I repeated. I was sure I must have heard him wrong. "For what?"

"You've opened my eyes to the evil nature of my master!" he replied.

"What are you talking about?" I asked.

"Did you see the way she treated you when she thought you were me?" Hundredeyes asked. "That old witch has always mistreated me, and she deserves a good punishment!"

I couldn't believe what I was hearing! I waited for Hundredeyes to tell me he was joking. But it didn't happen.

"You heard what she said, didn't you?" he continued. "*I'll talk to you later.*' Do you know what that means? It means she's planning to do to me what she did to her old assistant, Ludmilla. Circe turned her into a toad because she made one tiny mistake while she was preparing a potion!"

I turned toward the cave and saw that Becca

was already pointing her wand at Tyler. He cowered in fear.

"Please, brother, help me!" I begged. "I need something to light these with."

Maybe it was because he saw I was trying to help my friends, or maybe it was because I called him brother (as Aunt Harriet used to say, "Every bat is your brother"). Hundredeyes decided to help me.

"Okay," he said. "I think I remember the spell for the ring of fire."

"Oh, thank you!" I replied, almost in tears. "Thank you so much!"

Back in the cave, Becca was waving her wand in front of Tyler and starting to recite the first line of the spell.

"Darkness, lightning bolts, and fright . . ."

"So," Hundredeyes began, "if memory serves me, it goes something like this. *Sugar, eggs, honey, and flour* . . . no, that's a recipe for a cake! Let's see. It's right on the tip of my tongue . . ."

"Hurry up!" I said. "Faster! It's almost too late!"

Becca recited the second line.

"*Fill the air with hazy light . . .*"

"Oh, right . . ." Hundredeyes muttered. "*Fire, brimstone, jam on a scone* . . . crud, how did it go?"

Eyes blank, Becca went on:

"*Study the animals one by one . . .*"

"I've got it!" Hundredeyes exclaimed. He recited the whole spell in a single breath:

"Flames, blazes, sweltering heat,

Send us fire, brimstone, and peat!"

Suddenly, little flames started raining down on the smoke strings, setting them off just as Becca began to recite the last verse:

"And turn each into a pig . . ."

But before Becca could finish the sentence, the whole cave came alive with the most spectacular light show I had ever seen. Brightly colored strings and crazy circles of smoke whistled and darted around the cave. It made a huge mess, just as Michael had predicted.

The witch ran, screaming, to where Becca stood and tried to grab the wand away. But before the witch could do anything, Becca finished the spell herself: " . . . *just for fun!"*

Instantly, everything was engulfed in a cloud of white smoke. When Hundredeyes cleared the smoke using another spell he'd remembered (*Hazy mist, be scared of my fist!*), there was a big pink pig rooting around in the middle of the cave.

I almost fainted. Was that Tyler or Michael? But when I looked more closely, I realized that the pig was wearing a big pointy hat. It was Circe!

"Becca!" I shouted. She was standing next to the other girls, safe and sound. All three looked at each other, totally confused.

Then Becca saw me. "Echo!" she hollered, running toward me. I breathed a sigh of relief. She was finally free from the spell.

"Hey!" Tyler protested. "What about us?!" He and Michael were still sitting on the ground tied up.

Even Tyler's complaining couldn't bring me down. We were all there, alive and kicking. What a miracle! Or magic?

I looked at my watch. Midnight. The witching hour!

Chapter 13

The Great Hundredeyes

After we freed Michael and Tyler, everyone gathered on the island in the middle of the cave. The toads were strangely excited. They started croaking so loudly that we had to scream to introduce ourselves.

"MY NAME IS BECCA!" Becca hollered.

"I'M SARAH!" the short-haired girl yelled.

"I'M LAUREN!" the other one shouted.

"NICE TO MEET YOU!" Michael and Tyler yelled.

It was my turn. "MY NAME IS ECHO, AND THAT'S HUNDREDEYES!" I yelled, pointing to my cross-eyed friend.

The other two girls' mouths dropped open in shock. I understood. After all, a talking bat isn't something you see every day.

Hundredeyes waved his master's wand at the toads. "*ABSOLUTUM SILENTIUM!*" he said.

The toads instantly fell silent.

Now *everybody's* mouths fell open. I guess a cross-eyed bat wearing an orange hat that performs magic tricks *really* isn't something you see every day.

"I want to go home," Sarah said. "This place is creepy."

"Me too," Lauren added. "I want to see my family again."

"Well, I'd like to know what we're doing in a cave full of toads, pigs, and bats," Becca said, petting a huge brown toad.

"It's a long story," Michael said. "It's pretty similar to Snow White's, actually." He quickly told the girls what had happened, starting with the poison apples and ending with our rescue.

"You don't even remember how you turned the witch into a pig?" I asked Becca.

"You mean that's the witch?" she asked, pointing at the pig, which had its face in the muddy water.

"Yep," Michael answered. "That's her. When you said the last words of the spell, she tried to take the wand from you. She must have pointed it at herself instead."

"Could she break the spell?" I asked.

"The only way to break the spell is to say it backward," Hundredeyes told us.

"Well, as far as I know, there are no talking pigs. Only bats!" Tyler said cheerfully.

"Let's set her free in the Red Oak Wood," Michael suggested. "She'll find plenty of acorns, and she won't be able to hurt anyone."

"If you don't mind, I'd like to be the one to set her free," Hundredeyes said. He pointed the wand and shot a bolt of lightning at his former master. With a squeal, the pig that used to be Circe took off running and grunting toward the exit.

"Nice shot!" I told Hundredeyes.

"Well, it's all a matter of sight!" he said with a grin. "One last thing," Hundredeyes said. "I still have a friend I need to set free. Milla, come here!"

A sad-looking brown toad hopped toward him. Hundredeyes smiled at the toad and lightly touched it's head with the tip of the wand. From a cloud of golden sparks, a nice old lady appeared.

"This is Ludmilla," Hundredeyes said. "She was Circe's former assistant and my best friend!"

"Where is Circe now?" Ludmilla asked.

"Probably in the woods, looking for acorns," Tyler answered. "She was turned into a pig."

"Keep an eye on her, and never let her take on her original form," Hundredeyes said. Then he handed Ludmilla the wand. "Here. This belongs to you now."

The old lady took it and pointed it at the toads, mumbling something. We heard a funny noise — *POP! POP! POP!* — and the toads turned back into whoever they originally were. The cave was filled with boys and girls of every age. They were all victims of the evil witch, and were now being set free. Some of them stayed toads — well, I guess they always had been.

Chapter 14

Home Sweet Home

When we arrived home at three o'clock in the morning, it was quite a scene. Mrs. Silver wouldn't stop crying and hugging us, and Mr. Silver kept asking "Why do you smell like pigs?" and "Becca, what are you going to do with that toad?"

Finally, Mrs. Silver called the police and told them we were back. An hour later, Sarah and Lauren were taken back home to their families, safe and sound.

We kept the story we told the police as short as possible. (Some people just can't handle witches, magic wands, and talking bats!) We simply said that a crazy old lady had kidnapped the three girls, and that two brave brothers had rescued them. There was no trace of the old woman.

Since the sun was rising, Tyler demanded his breakfast. Our adventure had given him quite

an appetite. He looked like a hamster with his cheeks stuffed with food, and he was scattering food everywhere.

"Honestly, Tyler!" his mother said. "You eat like a pig!"

"Grunt! Grunt!" Tyler answered. "Exactly!"

* * *

A week later, Becca seemed to have gotten over the trauma of being kidnapped. She even asked me to help her with that school contest. We decided to write about a princess who, with the help of the dwarfs, opens a castle for princes who have been turned into toads. I think the judges are going to love it!

Hundredeyes and I have stayed friends after our adventure, even though I don't see him very much. But he did come to see me in my attic the other day. He invited me to a huge party he's planning. Now that he has the whole cave to himself, he wants to invite all the bats he knows!

I asked for his permission to tell our story. He said yes, on one condition. He wanted me to end the story by saying a director noticed his good looks and charming personality, and he became an actor. (Between you and me, I'm not sure I'm going to do it.)

I have to go now. I promised Michael that I would let him know what I thought about *The Revenge of the Giant Rabbit*, and I haven't even started it! Later I have to take Becca to the park. She wants to set the toad free in the pond. She insists that the bathtub isn't good enough for it.

See you next time!

A haunted goodbye from your friend,

ABOUT THE AUTHOR

Roberto Pavanello is an accomplished children's author and teacher. He currently teaches Italian at a local middle school and is an expert in children's theatre. Pavanello has written many children's books, including *Dracula and the School of Vampires*, *Look I'm Calling the Shadow Man!*, and the Bat Pat series, which has been published in Spain, Belgium, Holland, Turkey, Brazil, Argentina, China, and now the United States as Echo and the Bat Pack. He is also the author of the Oscar & Co. series, as well as the Flambus Green books. Pavanello currently lives in Italy with his wife and three children.

BOMBS AWAY!

Look closely at the two thieves — they're pretty familiar, aren't they? There are four differences between the first and second image. Can you tell what they are?

1.

2.

AEROBATIC LESSONS

While I was performing one of my night flights, I accidentally mixed up the steps! Can you help me put them back in the right order?

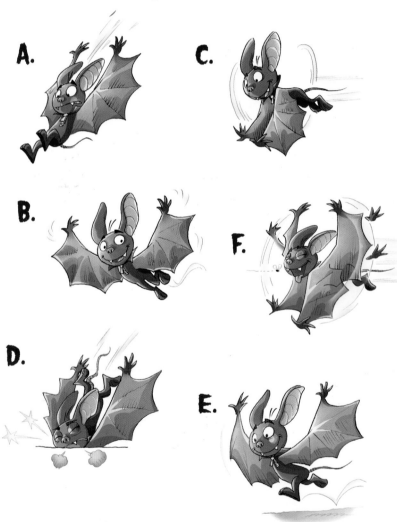

A.

C.

B.

F.

D.

E.

THE SOLITARY TOAD

Use your sonar! All of these toads have identical matches, except for one. Can you find the toad that has no match?

Check out more Mysteries and Adventures with Echo and the Bat Pack